Also by Joseph Pino

Nigel the Narwhal

Nigel the Narwhal Keeps Trying

Nicholas and the Narwhals
Keepers of the North Pole

by Joseph Pino

illustrations - John McNees

Nicholas and the Narwhals
Keepers of the North Pole
copyright © 2018 Joseph Pino

contact the author:
nigelthenarwhal@yahoo.com

ISBN - 13: 978-1790389544

illustration, cover and layout design by
John McNees / NOW Illustration and Design
copyright © 2018
nowillustrationanddesign.com
nowillustration@gmail.com

It was Christmas Eve, the sun had just set, and the house was filled with the smell of freshly baked cookies. Grandma had just put the grandkids to bed for the night, and grandpa entered the room to say his goodnights.

"Grandpa, grandpa, tell us a bedtime story! We're not tired yet!" pleaded the grandchildren.

1

"A story eh? Well… ok," teased grandpa with a twinkle in his eye. "I have the perfect story for you." He walked over to the bookshelf and pulled down a dusty, worn book that the kids had never seen before.

"This should do the trick, let me tell you the story of Nicholas and the Narwhals."

It all started in a time that has long slipped out of human memory.

In the North Pole, there lived a tribe of snow trolls known as the Gringozzle. They were not a nice bunch, in fact they were downright mean. They hated anything joyful or colorful, and their idea of fun was to make other people sad and miserable. They were short – only three feet tall – with white bodies shaped like bowling balls. They had stubby arms and legs, and heads that were long and thin, topped with spiky icicles for hair. Their mouths were filled with cracked and crooked teeth, and they looked at the world through eyes of cold, icy blue.

The Gringozzle only had one fear: water. If water ever came into contact with their skin it gave them the sensation of being tickled. They would laugh uncontrollably until ice tears rolled down their faces; so, as they hated anything joyous, it was their practice to avoid going near water.

3

The leader of the snow trolls was Queen Gringozzle, and in her possession was a crystal, known as the Arctic Crystal, which contained all the Magic of the North Pole. She was the iciest, grouchiest, and foulest of all the snow trolls; and her goal was to spread cold, misery, and sadness throughout the world. Each day, the Queen would pick three trolls, give them the Arctic Crystal, and command them to use the magic to make horrible winter storms. The magic was used to create huge icebergs that would clog up the sea, ice storms that would cover the lands, and snowstorms that could bury entire villages.

During these terrible winter storms people couldn't leave their homes to visit friends or family. Everything was dark and gray, and there was no color around to cheer them up. This caused people to have no joy to spread to others. It was a bad time, and the world had become a sad and lonely place to live.

4

It was during one of these terrible snowstorms that an adventurous young boy of ten, named Nicholas, ventured out to visit his grandmother. She was sick with a cold, and he felt it his duty to take her some soup and keep her company during the storm.

On the way to grandma's house, the lad became blinded and confused by all of the snow flying around and soon became lost. He stumbled around in the storm for a number of hours trying to find shelter, eventually coming upon a cave.

Deciding to wait out the storm, he went into the cave, started a small campfire with some twigs lying about, and settled in for the night.

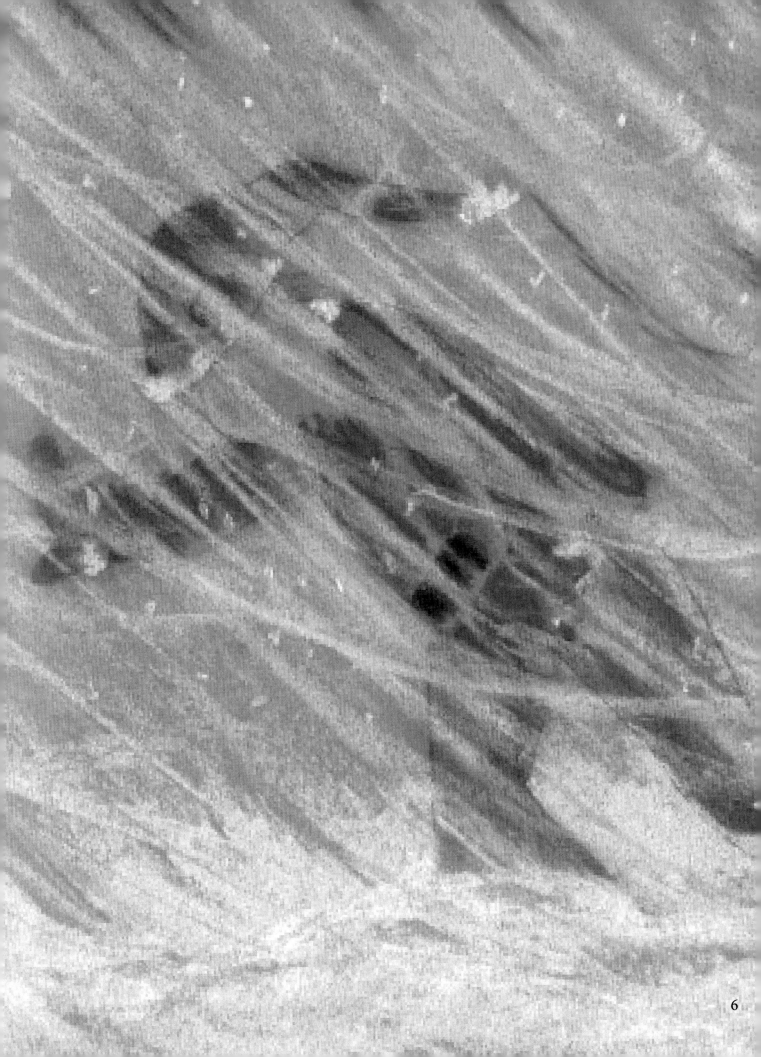

A short distance from where Nicholas camped, three Gringozzle – known as Darkly, Bluster, and Shiver – were outside with the Arctic Crystal. They were using the magic contained within the crystal to create the bleak, cold snowstorm that was currently hitting the area. The bickering of the Gringozzle could be heard between the gusts of wind.

"You've had it long enough Darkly, it's my turn!" said Bluster.

"No way Bluster, it's MY turn!" said Shiver. Both he and Bluster grabbed for the crystal and began pulling and fighting over it.

Just as their argument reached a fever pitch, the crystal popped out of their hands, flew over their heads, and landed out of sight in the growing snowdrift.

"Now you two have done it," scolded Darkly, "where did it go?"

"I don't see it!" cried Shiver.

"It's too snowy and dark!" added Bluster.

"You dunderheads. The Queen will banish us to the South Pole if we lose the crystal!" said Darkly. "Let's sneak back and not say anything. Tomorrow we'll get up early, come back out here and look for it."

8

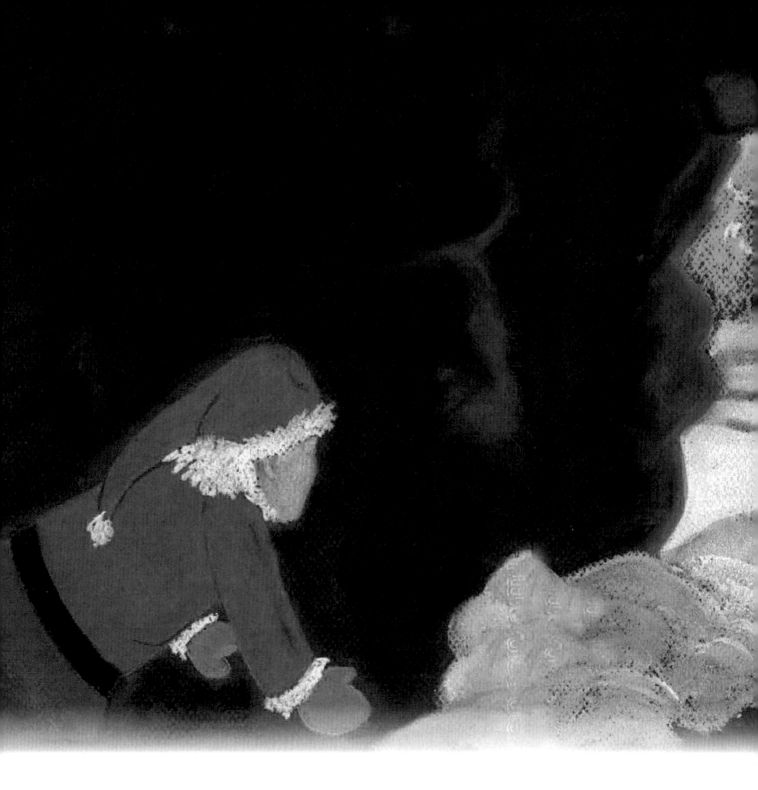

Nicholas woke the next morning with a large yawn and stretch, finding the mouth of the cave completely covered with snow. *Looks like I have some digging to do*, he thought.

He was cold, so he restarted the fire, and since he had the soup meant for grandma, he warmed it up and ate it for breakfast. Once he was done eating, he used his spoon and the bowl to start digging out of the cave.

Luckily for him, the snow wasn't packed down, and in no time he had dug himself out.

The view from outside the cave was beautiful, he could see fresh snow stretching out in all directions. Off to his right he could see the ocean, in front of him he could see a forest, and to his left the sun was still rising in the east. He didn't see any sign of his village, but knew that it lay east of the water. He started walking in that direction; all the while looking for any clues as to the location of his village.

Nicholas had only been walking for a short time when he caught sight of something in the snow; sparkling and reflecting the sunshine. "I wonder what that could be?" he asked himself as he clambered through the knee-deep snow at a faster pace.

He arrived at the object and wasn't sure what to make of it. Sticking halfway out of the freshly fallen snow was a crystal. It was about the length of a ruler, and as thick as his arm.

Nicholas picked it up to take a closer look.

The moment he touched the crystal, it was as if he had flipped on a light switch. Within the crystal itself, a spellbinding display of swirling colors came alive.

His world had been so gray and bleak that Nicholas had never seen such colors before. Witnessing such an array of colors in real life for the first time, he was filled with hope and happiness.

He thought that if he could somehow share this with others, they too would feel this joy. The flood of feelings anchored him to his spot as he stared into the crystal for a very long time.

Nicholas might have stayed there all day were it not for the braying sound of three approaching Gringozzle.

He shook himself out of his trance, shoved the crystal into his sack, and took off running to find a place to hide. Among the stories his grandma had shared, some were about the Gringozzle, and Nicholas was not interested in meeting them in person.

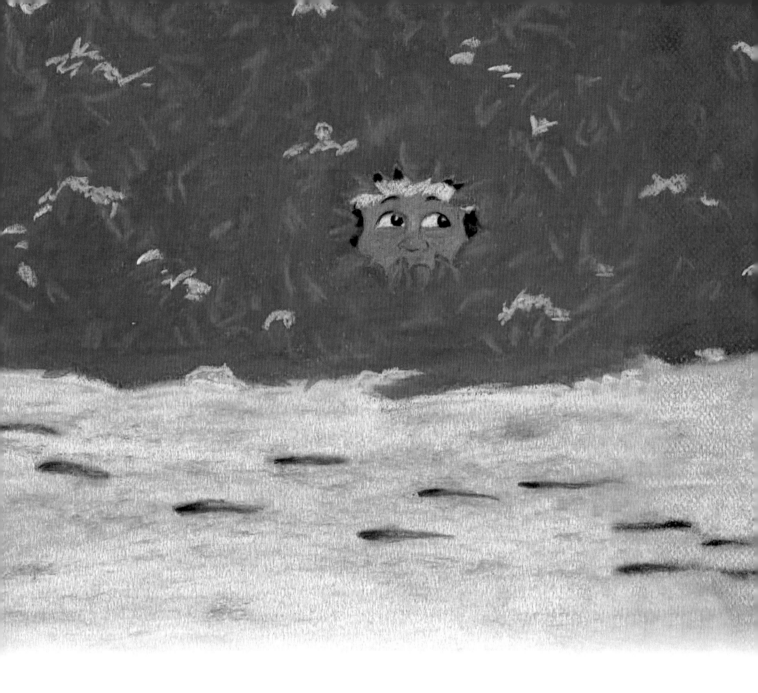

Nicholas quickly found a hiding place among a grouping of trees and bushes. He lay down among them and peeked out as the Gringozzle approached the spot where he had found the crystal.

"This is the area where we lost it, it should be here somewhere," said Shiver.

"There's a hole in the snow, maybe it was there," suggested Bluster.

"Yes, it was here, I can feel a small amount of leftover magic from the crystal," said Darkly.

Magic? thought Nicholas.

"Look here, footprints. I wonder if someone took our crystal," said Shiver.

"There's only one way to find out," said Bluster. The three Gringozzle set off to follow the footprints.

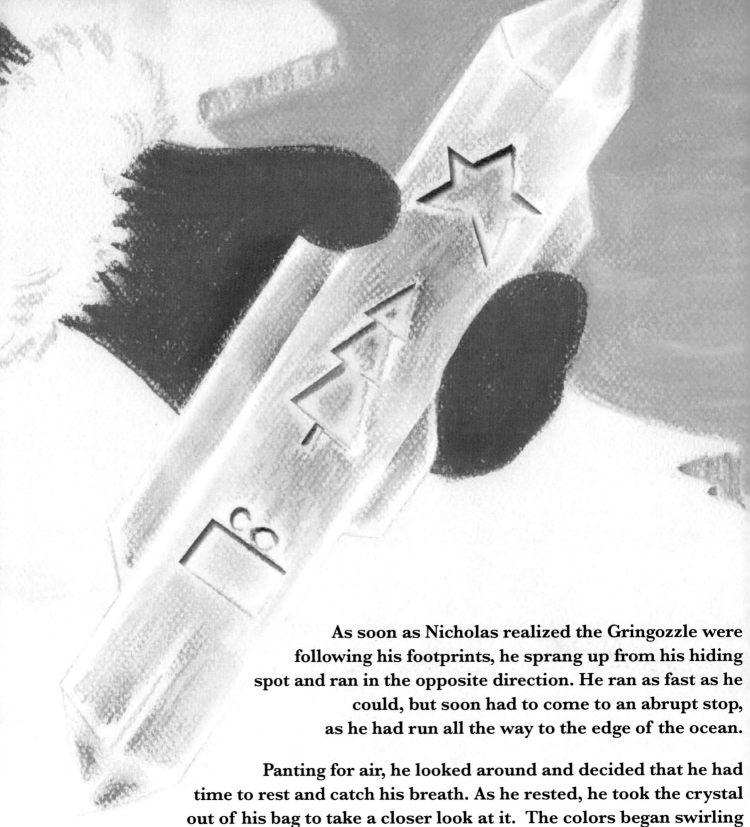

As soon as Nicholas realized the Gringozzle were following his footprints, he sprang up from his hiding spot and ran in the opposite direction. He ran as fast as he could, but soon had to come to an abrupt stop, as he had run all the way to the edge of the ocean.

Panting for air, he looked around and decided that he had time to rest and catch his breath. As he rested, he took the crystal out of his bag to take a closer look at it. The colors began swirling as wonderfully as before. Turning it over he noticed that there were symbols etched into it: a large star, a pine tree, and a box with a figure eight on top.

"I wonder what these symbols mean," pondered Nicholas aloud.

"I know what those mean," answered an unexpected voice from the water.

15

Nicholas shouted out in surprise. He looked up, expecting to see the Gringozzle.
Instead, a narwhal was bobbing on the surface of the water.

"Y-y-you're a narwhal! I've heard stories about you, but I never really believed that
you existed!" stammered Nicholas.

"Well, as you can see, narwhals are indeed real," chuckled the narwhal.

"I-I-I can hear you. You're talking! How is this possible? I must be dreaming!"
reasoned Nicholas.

"You're not dreaming, you and I can talk alright," said the narwhal. "The object you're holding is known as the Arctic Crystal. I'm surprised you've never heard of it, all of us arctic animals know about it. It is the reason you and I can talk to each other. Anyone holding the crystal has the Magic of the North Pole flowing through them. It's that magic that allows whoever is holding the crystal to talk with any arctic creature."

Nicholas was wide-eyed as he listened. He diverted his attention away from the narwhal as he heard a group of nearby penguins talking about what they were going to prepare for dinner that night. He looked in the other direction where he heard a couple of arctic foxes getting their den ready for some guests that were coming to visit. "Whoa," he whispered to himself.

Turning his attention back to the narwhal, Nicholas asked "So, do you know what these etchings mean?"

"Yes, I do. They are symbols for what the Magic of the North Pole embodies. The star symbolizes all of the stars in the sky, which remind us with their sparkling white light that there is light even in the darkest night.
The pine tree symbolizes all of the evergreen trees in the world, these remind us with their vibrant green that hope remains even during the coldest days.
The last symbol is a gift box, this reminds us with its colorful wrapping that joy is best shared with those who are in need," explained the narwhal.

"Why don't we have any of these things in the world?" asked Nicholas.

"Sadly, the Gringozzle stole the crystal long ago. It has been under their control ever since. There are very few people who remember such nice things," answered the narwhal.

"That's awful! I'm going to make sure those trolls never get this back."
Just then Nicholas heard murmuring and twigs snapping in the near distance.

"Oh no! The Gringozzle are here! I can't let this fall back into their hands, but there's no place to hide!" said Nicholas.

"I have an idea," said the narwhal. "As you probably know, Gringozzle avoid water."

"Oh yeah, I remember my grandma telling me that once," replied Nicholas.

"Well, there's a small island not far from here, climb on my back and I'll swim you over to it!" suggested the narwhal.

"Then we'll be safe from the Gringozzle since we'll be surrounded by water! That's a great idea!" Nicholas grabbed his bag, waded into the water, and climbed onto the narwhal's back.

"Hold on tight," said the narwhal and off they went.

19

As Nicholas and the narwhal sped off to the safety of the island, the Gringozzle stumbled out of the woods, watching as Nicholas rode away.

"No! Our crystal!" they cried out in unison.

"Now what are we going to do?!" cried Bluster.

"Ahhh! Water!" exclaimed Shiver, backing away from the edge of the water.

"Well, we know one thing for sure, the kid isn't going anywhere. It's time we told the Queen, she'll know what to do," said Darkly.

"Well, since you're giving me a ride, I should introduce myself, my name is Nicholas," said the boy.

"Pleased to meet you Nicholas, my name is Finn," replied the narwhal.

They soon arrived at the island. Finn swam up close to the island and Nicholas slid off his back onto the rocky shore. "This place is great," said Nicholas as he surveyed the land. The island's shore was made up of small, rounded black stones that sparkled in the sun. The island was as big as two soccer fields, with a number of pine trees spread around. In the very center of the island was the largest crystal rock formation he had ever seen. "Wow, that's amazing!" proclaimed Nicholas.

"It sure is. It's known as Quartz Castle," said Finn.

"I can see why, it does look like a castle. It's so cool!" Nicholas stepped up to the formation and put his hand out to touch it. Suddenly he slipped, the Arctic Crystal fell out of his hand and landed upon Quartz Castle. When the two came into contact, the entire castle lit up with the same swirling colors locked inside the Arctic Crystal! The sky above the island was bathed in wavy, swirling colors, as if Nicholas was standing inside a giant kaleidoscope!

Staring in wonder at the colorful display, Nicholas took a few steps backward, slipping once again; this time he fell onto his back. His foot struck the Arctic Crystal and broke the connection with Quartz Castle. The spectacular light show blinked out and ended just as abruptly as it had started. "What just happened Finn?" asked Nicholas.

Finn was just bobbing there wide-eyed, "I-I-I don't believe it. The-the legend is true!" stammered Finn.

"What legend?" asked Nicholas.

"It has been said that a human with a heart of pure joy could bring together the Arctic Crystal and the Quartz Castle to release and magnify the Magic of the North Pole held within. Quartz Castle is large enough to spread the Magic of the North Pole throughout the world, dispel the gray, and restore the joy and happiness that has been lost for so long. Nicholas, YOU are that person!"

While Nicholas continued to explore the island, Bluster, Shiver, and Darkly had returned to tell the Queen what had happened. She was angry that they had lost the Arctic Crystal, and deep down was worried that the crystal would be lost forever, ending her rule. She commanded the three Gringozzle to lead her to the spot where the boy was last seen. As Queen Gringozzle and her trolls approached the location where Nicholas and the narwhal swam off, she was blinded by the bright blast of color that had appeared from the distant island.

"No!" she cried "It can't be! It's just a made-up legend, a story that humans tell at bedtime!" Upon seeing the blast of color, Bluster, Shiver, and Darkly huddled together babbling and sobbing with fright.

23

"Wh-wh-what are we going to do?!" the three Gringozzle asked in unison.

"I'll tell you what we're going to do, you three knuckleheads are going to start chopping down trees and build a bridge to that island immediately!" commanded the Queen.

"Yes, your majesty!" shouted the Gringozzle as they bumped and stepped over each other, hurrying over to the woods to get started.

"We're going to need every Gringozzle for this task," said the Queen as she pulled out her horn and blew a note to summon the rest of her trolls.

The call of the horn caught Nicholas's attention. He squinted at the growing group of Gringozzle, "What do you think they're up to?"

"I don't know, but it can't be good," replied Finn.

As the Gringozzle splashed the first log into the sea, Nicholas realized what they were doing. "Oh no! They're building a bridge to the island! What are we going to do?" asked Nicholas.

"I have an idea. I'm going to go get some help." Finn said as he dived down into the water.

All Nicholas could do was wait and watch as the Gringozzle continued splashing more and more logs into the sea; the bridge getting closer and closer. Nicholas looked around, but there was no place to hide on the island, he just hoped that help would get there soon.

The bridge was soon complete and the Gringozzle began walking on it toward the island. "You have nowhere to hide now little boy!" shrieked the Queen, who remained on shore. "The Arctic Crystal belongs to me, and soon my trolls will get it back."

Nicholas scurried up Quartz Castle as high as he could, but it was no use. Darkly, Bluster, Shiver, and the rest of the Gringozzle were soon on the island and right on his heels. They stood on each other's shoulders, forming a ladder of Gringozzle. Shiver, at the top of the ladder, grabbed him by his ankles and carried him back down to the ground.

"I think you have something that belongs to the Queen," growled Bluster as he grabbed Nicholas's backpack. He opened the bag, reached in, and pulled out the crystal. Upon being seized by the Gringozzle, the Arctic Crystal turned dull and gray.

"We have it Your Majesty!" cried out Darkly and Shiver in unison.

"Don't just stand there, bring it to me!" shouted the Queen.

The Gringozzle scurried about for a moment, bumping into each other, before finally organizing themselves to cross back over the bridge.

Nicholas just sat watching, he couldn't believe what just happened. The Gringozzle had the crystal back, and now he wouldn't be able to share with the world the amazing colors and joy it contained.

"I can't watch," sobbed Nicholas. Tears formed in his eyes as he turned away from the Gringozzle, who were now halfway back to shore.

As he turned, he caught sight of a tusk emerging from the water. It was Finn!
Another tusk emerged next to him, then another, and another! As Nicholas stood
up, he guessed there must have been forty or fifty narwhals.

"They have the crystal, Finn! They're going to give it back to the Queen!"
exclaimed Nicholas.

"Not if we have anything to say about it," replied Finn. "Let's go narwhals, just as
we planned!"

The narwhals quickly swam toward the bridge, spread themselves out one fin apart, and formed a long line the length of the bridge.

"What are those…narwhals? No!" cried out the Queen. She began to warn her army to watch out, but it was too late. The narwhals stuck their tusks into the logs and began to roll them back and forth.

The Gringozzle quickly lost their balance and began plopping into the water. The sound of Gringozzle squealing and laughing soon filled the air.

"Great job narwhals!" exclaimed Nicholas, jumping excitedly up and down. His tears of sadness were replaced with those of relief and laughter.

Bluster was the final Gringozzle on the bridge, "I'm almost there," he grunted as he lumbered onto the final log. Finn rushed up and gave the log a mighty wallop, shaking Bluster, which made him lose his balance and forced the crystal to fly out of his hand!

As the crystal was about to splash into the water, a tusk emerged and poked it back into the air. Gravity pulled on the crystal, and a second tusk poked it up into the sky again. The narwhals were playing catch with the crystal, moving it closer to the island by poking it one by one back into the air, ensuring that it didn't fall into the water!

Nicholas watched all of this in amazement. He noticed that each time the Arctic Crystal made contact with a tusk, the tusk lit up with the same kaleidoscope of lights that he had seen in the crystal. *Interesting*, thought Nicholas.

The narwhal closest to the island gave the crystal one final poke high into the sky and Nicholas jumped up and grabbed it. "Got it!" he shouted.

As the Gringozzle slowly swam back to the mainland, out of breath and sore from so much laughing, the Queen shouted at Nicholas, "Aaarrghhh! You may have the Arctic Crystal for now, but I'll never stop trying to get it back. The world belongs in a blanket of gray!"

Finn and four other narwhals silently swam up to the Queen as she was shouting. They turned their backs toward her and said "Hey Queen, we think it's time for you to chill out!" then they slapped the water with their tails, creating a wave of frigid water that completely drenched the Queen. She fell to the ground, holding her stomach and laughing uncontrollably.

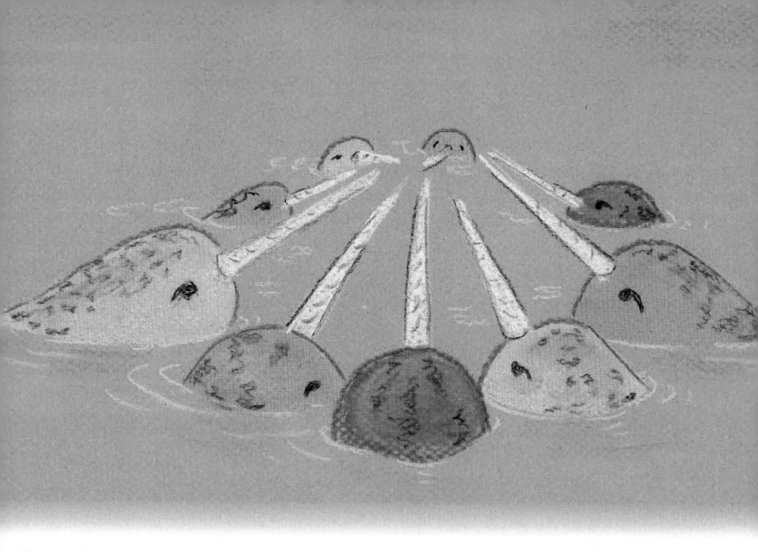

Finn and the narwhals swam back to the island and met Nicholas at the water's edge.

"That was amazing you guys! Thank you so much for getting the crystal back," said Nicholas.

"You're welcome, the Gringozzle have controlled the crystal for too long," replied Finn.

"So, now that we have it, how do we keep it safe? You heard the Queen, she'll never stop trying to get it back," worried Nicholas.

"Hmm, that is a doozy of a question," said Finn. "Any ideas guys?" he asked the other narwhals.

The narwhals formed a circle and put their tusks together, Nicholas could hear whispering but couldn't make out what they were saying. After a few minutes, one of the narwhals swam out of the circle and whispered something to Finn. Finn listened and nodded.

"Nicholas, we have an idea: keep the crystal on the island! The water is a natural defense, also we narwhals volunteer to constantly guard the island and keep an eye on it," explained Finn.

"That's very kind of you, but the Gringozzle are tricky. Even with you guarding the island I'm worried about leaving the crystal out in the open. If there was only a way to lock it away safely," replied Nicholas. Slowly, a smile started to form on Nicholas's face.

"Wait a minute…I have an idea. Did you notice what happened when you and the rest of the narwhals touched the crystal with your tusk?"

"Well, no, we were too busy watching the crystal, making sure it didn't fall into the water," replied Finn.

"Each time the crystal made contact with a narwhal tusk, the tusk lit up with the colors of the crystal! I think I can empty the magic contained in the Arctic Crystal into your tusk! That way it would always be safe, in the water with you and the rest of the narwhals!" said Nicholas gleefully.

"I don't know Nicholas, the Magic of the North Pole is very important, are you sure you want to entrust it to me and the narwhals?" questioned Finn.

"Absolutely! You've helped me so much, and the narwhals were so brave standing up to the Gringozzle! I can't think of a better keeper of the magic," assured Nicholas.

"Well… ok. Let's do it!" agreed Finn.

Finn swam up to the shore of the island and rested his head on the rocky beach. Nicholas walked over and met him at the shoreline. They looked at each other a moment, nodded, then Nicholas touched the crystal to the tip of Finn's tusk. The magical colors started shining instantly; red, blue, green, yellow, silver, gold, purple. The colors began to drain out of the crystal and flow down into Finn's tusk. After only a few seconds, the transfer was done. The crystal was now just an ordinary white crystal, but Finn's tusk was a constantly swirling display of colors!

"It worked!" exclaimed Nicholas, "how do you feel?"

"I feel great! Happy, strong, and hopeful; but mostly I feel honored," said Finn. "Let's celebrate! I'll invite all of the arctic animals to celebrate freeing the Magic of the North Pole!"

"That sounds great, but...my family is probably worried about me and wondering where I am. I should head back home," said Nicholas, as he noticed the sun was beginning to set.

"Oh, I guess you're right," said Finn glumly. "When will we get to see you again? When will we get to share the magic with the world?"

"How about tomorrow? I can't wait to celebrate and release those joyful colors throughout the world!" suggested Nicholas.

"Tomorrow's December 25th, that sounds great to us!" answered Finn and the narwhals.

"Terrific! Tomorrow we'll celebrate defeating the Gringozzle and freeing the Magic of the North Pole. We'll use the magic in your tusk along with the Quartz Castle to blast out a huge dose of magic that will cover the entire world with color, hope, and joy!" declared Nicholas.

"We love it!" agreed the narwhals.

"From this day forward, the narwhals promise to be the Keepers of the Magic of the North Pole, protect the magic, and help you spread the joy and hope that it contains." declared Finn.

"And that's just what they did," said grandpa as he closed the book. "Each year, on December 25th, Nicholas and the narwhals meet at Quartz Castle and release the Magic of the North Pole for the world to enjoy."

"Over time, they started giving one another little gifts to express how much they cared for each other. Eventually, unable to contain their joy to just the island, they used some of the magic to create a workshop. It's at this workshop where gifts are made to share with all of the good boys and girls of the world."

"Speaking of which," said grandpa looking at the clock, "you'd better get to sleep if you don't want our house to be skipped by Nicholas this year."

Yawning, the grandchildren thanked grandpa for the story and began to settle in for the night.

"Grandpa?" asked one of the grandchildren. "Is that story really true? The narwhals, Nicholas, the Magic of the North Pole?"

"Well my dear, I know that I'm more joyous and my heart feels lighter this time each year." replied grandpa, as he looked out the window, a smile playing across his mouth. "Ultimately it's something you'll have to decide for yourselves."

As grandpa turned and walked out of the bedroom, the grandchildren looked to where his gaze had fallen. Outside the window a wavy, colorful, magical light could be seen in the near distance.

About the Author

Joseph Pino is the son of Italian immigrants who came to America in the early 1970s. He's had a lifelong fascination with whales, particularly the narwhal, when he learned about them in his sixth-grade science class. He currently lives in Michigan with his wife and their two children.

Made in the USA
Lexington, KY
20 December 2018